July 1994

To my Koshka Arthur
   my tallest tall tallest tree
   in the biggest desert.
      i love you
         ♡ love Amy

Wendal, His Cat, and the Progress of Man

an illustrated novel

by

v. campudoni

LONGSTREET PRESS
Atlanta, Georgia

To Eva, Elizabeth,
and Moo Goo

Published by LONGSTREET PRESS, INC.,
a subsidiary of Cox Newspapers,
a division of Cox Enterprises, Inc.
2140 Newmarket Parkway
Suite 118
Marietta, Georgia 30067

Printed in the United States of America

1st printing, 1994

ISBN: 1-56352-128-8

This book was printed by Arcata Graphics, Kingsport, Tennessee.

Jacket and book design by Laura McDonald

Wendal, His Cat, and the Progress of Man

Wendal Worked

Wendal worked in a very small office surrounded by a very big civilization called mankind. Mankind was constantly on the move and forever progressing, and Wendal's job, in this civilization, was to do nothing.

Wendal did nothing and he did it well. Wendal worked hard at doing nothing and hard work was a virtue.

Wendal's inspiration to work hard was his boss. Wendal's boss was a fine man with many great qualities and a zest for life. Wendal's boss would say things like, "I need you, Wendal," and, "Can I give you another raise, Wendal?" Sometimes Wendal's boss would just sit in his office and think of ways to make Wendal's life easier.

During his lunch break Wendal would go to his favorite restaurant where the restaurant worker would say, "Hi! What can I do for you?" and, "Have a great day!" and, "One day I'm going to burn this place down with everyone in it."

After a hearty meal Wendal would go to the park and watch the children play. Wendal was captured by their innocence and charm and believed they were the future of mankind.

While he was at the park Wendal would visit the tree.
Wendal liked the tree because it made him feel like he was
part of a living, breathing planet, vibrating with energy and
pulsating with a great life force that surrounded everything,
everywhere. Wendal's tree was big and strong and proof that
life — in spite of the never-ending march of civilization and
the progress of man — was the most powerful, and most
sacred, thing in the universe.

After lunch Wendal would return to work.

And after work Wendal would go home.

At home Wendal did many things. But mostly Wendal would watch television. Wendal was quite fond of situation comedies involving hilarity and tense police action dramas. Wendal also enjoyed watching the news. Wendal liked the news because it kept him informed on the never-ending march of civilization and the progress of man.

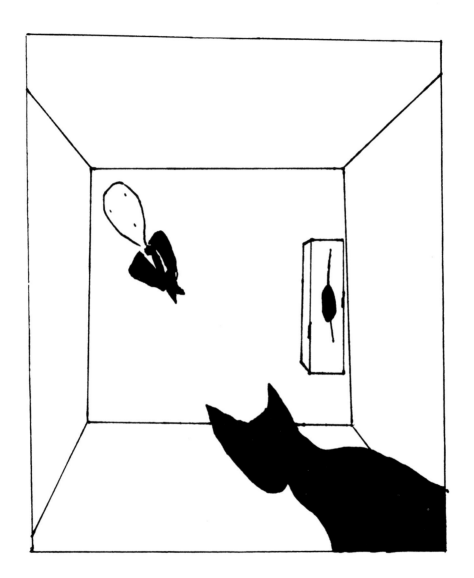

Wendal also had a cat.

Gai Pan

Gai Pan was small and dark and loved to play all day long. Sometimes she would pounce on Wendal's head and Wendal would say, "Ouch," or, "Stop that, cat," but Gai Pan would not stop. In fact, when Wendal was not in the mood to play, Gai Pan wanted to play even more. Gai Pan also liked to race around the house and make Wendal dizzy. "Stop that, cat," Wendal would say, but Gai Pan, of course, would not stop.

One day Gai Pan began to watch television. During the situation comedy Gai Pan asked Wendal, "Why are those people bleeding?" and Wendal said, "Because someone has stabbed them repeatedly." And during the tense police action drama Gai Pan asked Wendal, "Why are those people bleeding?" and Wendal said, "Because someone has stabbed them repeatedly." And during the news Gai Pan asked Wendal, "Why are those people bleeding?" and Wendal said, "Because someone has stabbed them repeatedly."

After many hours of television Gai Pan sat and stared at Wendal.

"Is everything OK?" Wendal asked Gai Pan.

Gai Pan said nothing.

The next day Gai Pan remained silent.

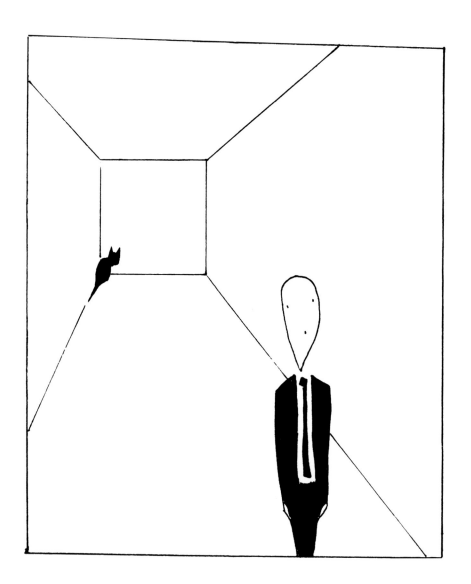

And the day after that.

After three days of silence Gai Pan spoke:

"Wendal," she said, "what kind of world do we live in?"

Wendal said nothing.

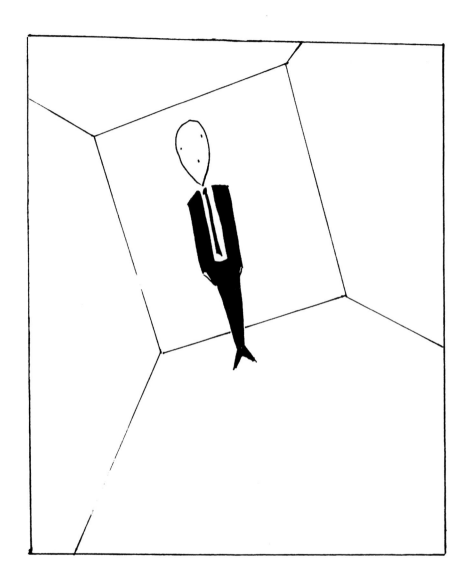

The next day Wendal returned from work and could not find Gai Pan.

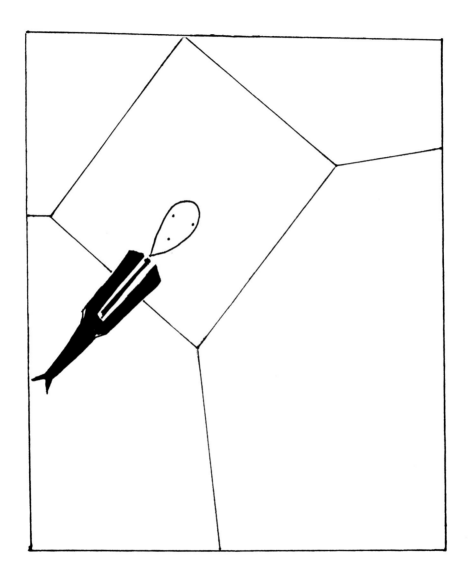

He looked everywhere . . .

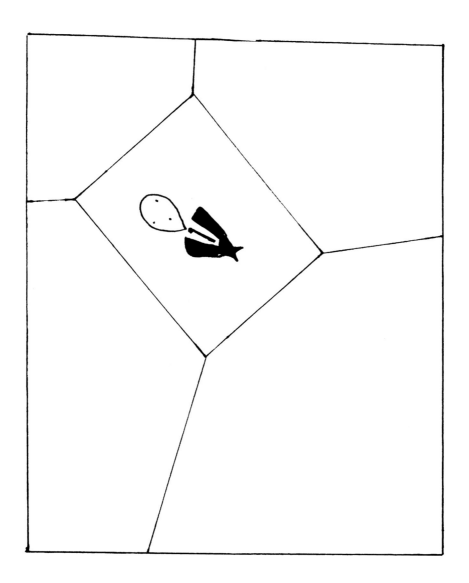

. . . and everywhere.

Wendal became very concerned and decided to ask his neighbor if he had seen Gai Pan.

"What do you want?" asked the neighbor.

"Hello, my name is Wendal and I was wondering if you had seen my cat."

"Who are you?" asked the neighbor.

"I am your friendly neighbor," said Wendal, "and I was wondering if you had seen my cat. She is small and dark and loves to play all day long."

"What do you want?" asked the neighbor.

"I was wondering if you had seen my cat. Her name is . . ."

"I am now going to kill you," said Wendal's neighbor.

It was clear to Wendal that his neighbor was much too busy studying the progress of man and was not concerned with little lost cats. Wendal then decided to call the police and ask them to help him find his cat.

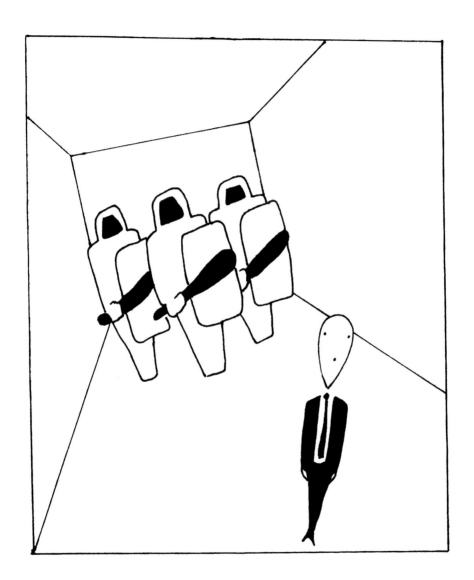

"Where is the riot?" asked the police.

"There is no riot," said Wendal. "I have called you because I have lost my cat and I was hoping that you might help me find her."

"Where are the bodies?" asked the police.

"There are no bodies," said Wendal. "I have simply lost my cat. Her name is Gai Pan and she is small and dark."

"Where are those who wish to be beaten senseless?"

"There is no one here who wishes to be beaten," said Wendal. "I have lost my cat."

"Are you planning to start a riot?" asked the police.

"No," said Wendal.

"Call us when there is rampage and murder," said the police.

"Very well," said Wendal.

It was clear to Wendal that the police were much too busy protecting the never-ending march of civilization and could not be expected to search for little lost cats. Wendal decided to go to his church and ask the preacher to help him find his cat.

"Did you come to bring me money?" asked the preacher.

"No," said Wendal. "I have lost my cat and I was hoping that you would help me find her."

"How much money do you have?" asked the preacher.

"I do not have much money," said Wendal. "I have lost my cat and I was hoping that you would help me find her. She is small and dark and loves to play all day long."

"Let's talk about money, shall we?" asked the preacher.

"Perhaps if I were to stand on top of your church I would see her in the distance," said Wendal.

"Give me money," said the preacher.

"I have none," said Wendal.

"Go away," said the preacher.

It was clear to Wendal that the preacher was much too busy saving souls and could not be expected to be concerned with little lost cats. But Wendal had another idea: he would call the television news people and ask them to help him find his cat.

"Tell us about the blood and carnage," asked the television news man.

"There is no blood and carnage," said Wendal. "There is only my lost cat."

"Tell us about the death and destruction," asked the television news man.

"There is no death and destruction," said Wendal. "I have lost my cat. Her name is Gai Pan."

"Tell us about those who were killed and how well you knew them and what good people they were and how tragic this all seems."

"I have simply lost my cat," said Wendal.

"Tell us about their agony, tell us about the screaming and their cries for help. Tell us about how no one listened and no one cared as their lives were being snuffed out."

"No one has been killed," said Wendal.

"Tell us about how cheap life has become."

"Perhaps," said Wendal.

It was clear to Wendal that the television news man was much more concerned with the progress of man than with little lost cats.

The next day Wendal went to work.

Wendal's boss noticed that Wendal was not himself and called him into his office.

"Is everything OK?" asked Wendal's boss.

"No," said Wendal. "I have lost my cat and I cannot find her."

"Say no more, my good friend. I know exactly how you feel."

"Do you?"

"Yes," said Wendal's boss, "I love cats."

"Really?" asked Wendal.

"Of course," said Wendal's boss. "I had a cat once when I was a child. I very much enjoyed playing with her. Sometimes I would spin her around by her tail very quickly, then release her and watch her go flying across the yard. Sometimes I would take a hammer and pound on her head until she blacked out. Once I drove a nail into her skull and after that she was never quite the same."

Wendal said nothing.

"Wendal, I would like to buy you another cat. But you must promise me one thing."

"What?" asked Wendal.

"That you would let me play with it," said Wendal's boss.

Wendal said nothing.

When lunchtime came Wendal went to his favorite restaurant, only to find that it had been burned to the ground.

And Wendal went to the park and saw one of the children.

"Where are your friends?" asked Wendal.

"I have killed them all," said the child.

Wendal then went to visit the tree and found that his tree, the tree that had made him feel like he was part of a living, breathing planet, vibrating with energy and pulsating with a great life force that surrounded everything, everywhere, the tree that was big and strong and proof that life — in spite of the never-ending march of civilization and the progress of man — was the most powerful, and most sacred, thing in the universe, had been cut down.

And Wendal grew tired.

And Wendal thought about the world that he lived in.

And Wendal stood up.

The Progress of Man

Wendal went to see his boss.

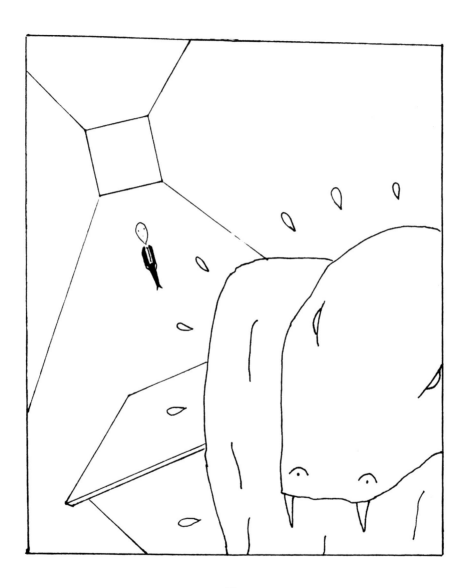

"Excuse me, sir," said Wendal.

"Yes?" said Wendal's boss.

"May we speak?" asked Wendal.

"Of course," said Wendal's boss. "What's on your mind?"

"Well, sir," said Wendal, "I was thinking about how you played with your cat."

"And?"

"And . . . well . . . it seems to me that spinning a cat around by its tail . . . is . . . cruel."

"Cruel?" asked Wendal's boss. "Cruel in what sense?"

"It is cruel, sir, in the sense that it is wrong."

"Wrong?" asked Wendal's boss.

"Wrong," said Wendal.

"Wendal," said Wendal's boss, "we're talking about a cat, right?"

"Yes," said Wendal, "and it is also wrong to take a hammer and pound on its little head."

"It was a cat, Wendal, a cat."

"And driving a nail into its skull is absolutely inhuman," said Wendal.

"A cat," said Wendal's boss.

"Yes," said Wendal, "a cat."

"They live for that sort of stuff," said Wendal's boss.

"No, they don't," said Wendal. "Nothing lives to be treated like that."

"Wendal," said Wendal's boss, "I am going to give you a raise. Would you like that?"

"No," said Wendal. "In fact, I don't think I wish to work here anymore."

"Why?" asked Wendal's boss.

And Wendal went back to his neighbor's home.

"Who are you?" asked Wendal's neighbor.

"I am Wendal," said Wendal, "and I am your neighbor and you are mine. I have lost my cat and I was wondering if you had seen her. She is small and dark."

"What do you want?" asked the neighbor.

"I have just told you," said Wendal. "I have lost my cat and I wish to know whether you have seen her or not."

"Who are you?" asked the neighbor.

"You are not listening to me," said Wendal.

"I am now going to kill you," said Wendal's neighbor.

"No," said Wendal. "You are not going to kill me or anything else on this planet."

"Who are you?" asked the neighbor.

"I am your neighbor," said Wendal.

"What do you want?" asked the neighbor.

Wendal then went back to the church.

"Did you come to bring me money?" asked the preacher.

"No," said Wendal. "I have lost my cat and I was hoping that you would help me find her."

"Do you have any money?" asked the preacher.

"That is not important," said Wendal. "What is important is that I need help and you must help me."

"Nonsense," said the preacher.

"Take me to the top of this church," said Wendal.

"There is nothing up there," said the preacher.

"This church is very tall; perhaps I will see her in the distance."

"No," said the preacher.

"You must," said Wendal.

"What is it worth to you?"

"Everything," said Wendal.

"Will you give me money?" asked the preacher.

"I will give you everything I have," said Wendal.

"What are we waiting for? Let's go."

And Wendal went to the top of the church to find his cat.

"I cannot see her," said Wendal. "Can you?"

"I see nothing," said the preacher, "nor do I care to see anything."

"Do you care only about money?" asked Wendal.

"Of course," said the preacher. "Money is the most important thing in the universe."

"I think not," said Wendal.

"You are insane," said the preacher.

"And you are a criminal," said Wendal.

"How dare you?" said the preacher. "Do you know who you're talking to?"

"Yes," said Wendal, "I am supposed to be talking to someone who is kind and compassionate, someone who teaches and enlightens, someone who shows us the way through the darkness. But instead I am talking to a criminal. One who counts money while the world bleeds around him."

"How dare you," said the preacher. "You will leave my church right now."

"This is not your church," said Wendal.

"I will call the police," said the preacher.

"Call them," said Wendal.

And the police arrived.

And so did the television news man.

"Where is the riot?" asked the police.

"I am the riot," said Wendal.

"Tell us about the blood and carnage," said the television news man.

"It is everywhere," said Wendal.

"Do you wish to be beaten senseless?" asked the police.

"Nothing that lives would wish violence upon itself," said Wendal.

"Tell us about the death and destruction," said the television news man.

"That too is everywhere," said Wendal.

"Tell us about how cheap life has become," said the television news man.

"Life," said Wendal, "is sacred."

"Prepare to be beaten and bludgeoned," said the police.

"Wait," said the preacher. "I have a better idea."

And Wendal was nailed to the cross.

And as he hung on the cross Wendal looked out into the distance. Wendal saw his home and the park and the place where he had worked, and beyond. Wendal saw riots and bleeding and rampage and murder; Wendal saw lies and greed and a great darkness that had come to possess mankind. And then Wendal looked up into the sky. And Wendal saw Gai Pan.

"Can you hear me, Wendal?" Gai Pan asked.

"Yes," said Wendal, "I can."

"I'm sorry I've caused you such worry," said Gai Pan. "Forgive me."

"Everything is well," said Wendal. "I have found you."

"I would like to take you somewhere," said Gai Pan.

"I cannot move," said Wendal.

"Yes, you can," said Gai Pan. "You are freer now than you have ever been before. Follow me."

And Gai Pan took Wendal across time, space, and all of eternity, and to the very end of the world.

"This is my tree," said Gai Pan. "Do you like it?"

"Yes," said Wendal, "it is very beautiful."

"And it is part of a living, breathing planet," said Gai Pan, "that vibrates with energy and pulsates with a great life force that surrounds everything, everywhere."

"It is very big," said Wendal.

"And it is strong," said Gai Pan, "and proof that life — in spite of the never-ending march of civilization and the progress of man — is the most powerful, and most sacred, thing in the universe."

And Wendal smiled.